TIMEPOCALYPSE #2

ABDO
Spotlight

DARK
HORSE
COMICS

PopCap

Written by **PAUL TOBIN**
Art by **RON CHAN**
Colors by **MATTHEW J. RAINWATER**
Letters by **STEVE DUTRO**
Cover by **RON CHAN**

President and Publisher **MIKE RICHARDSON**
Editor **PHILIP R. SIMON**
Assistant Editor **ROXY POLK**
Designer **KAT LARSON**
Digital Production **CHRISTINA McKENZIE**

Special thanks to LEIGH BEACH, SHANA DOERR, A.J. RATHBUN, BRENNAN TOWNLEY, JEREMY VANHOOZER, and everyone at PopCap Games.

DarkHorse.com | PopCap.com

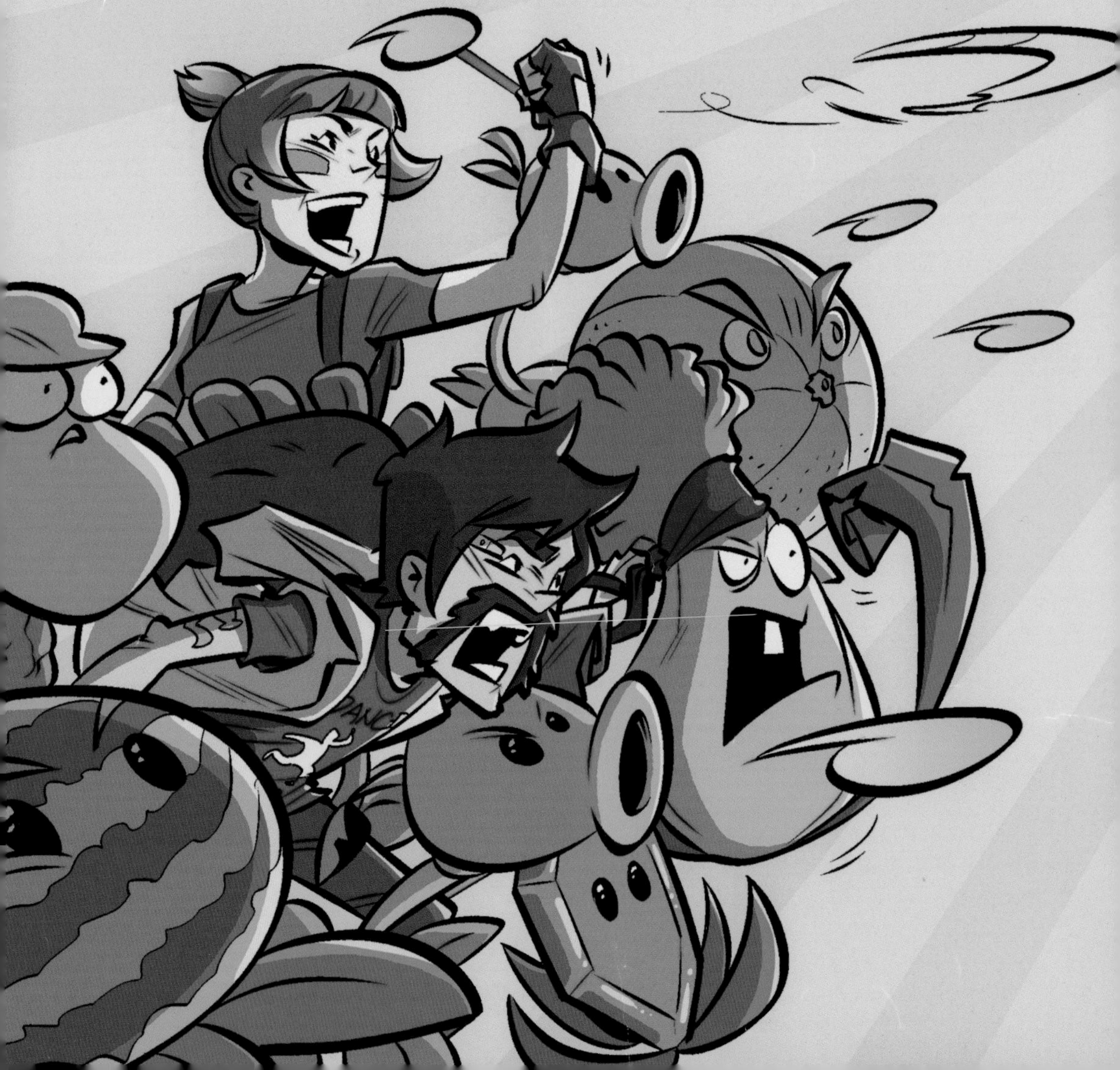

PLANTS VS. ZOMBIES™

TIMEPOCALYPSE #2

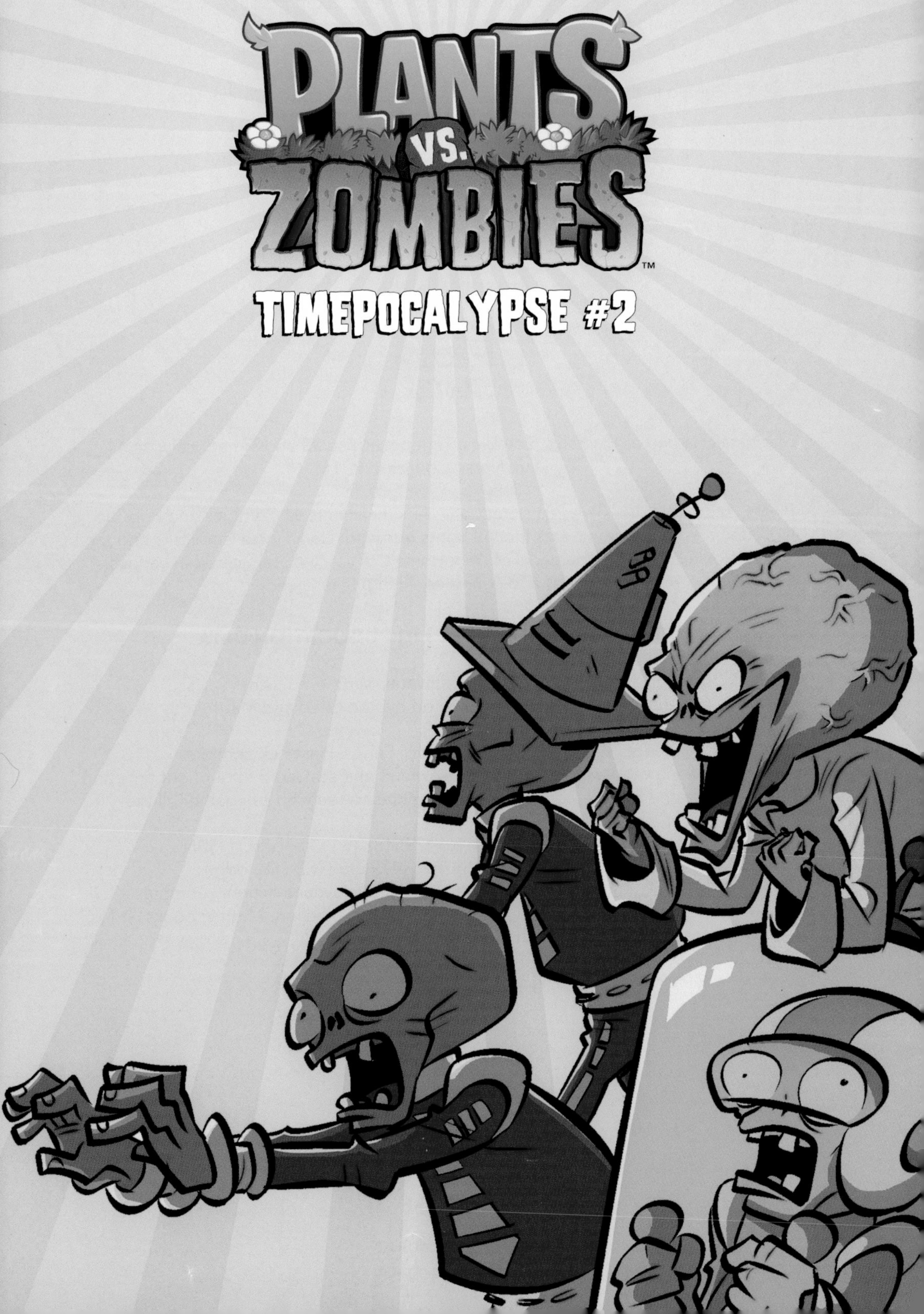

ABDOPUBLISHING.COM

Reinforced library bound edition published in 2017 by Spotlight, a division of ABDO, PO Box 398166, Minneapolis, Minnesota 55439. Spotlight produces high-quality reinforced library bound editions for schools and libraries.
Published by agreement with Dark Horse Comics.

Printed in the United States of America, North Mankato, Minnesota.
042016
092016

THIS BOOK CONTAINS
RECYCLED MATERIALS

Originally issued as Plants vs. Zombies: Timepocalypse #3 and Timepocalypse #4 by Dark Horse Comics in 2014.

PUBLISHER'S CATALOGING IN PUBLICATION DATA

Names: Tobin, Paul, author. | Chan, Ron ; Rainwater, Matthew J., illustrators.
Title: Timepocalypse / by Paul Tobin ; illustrated by Ron Chan and Matthew J. Rainwater.
Description: Minneapolis, MN : Spotlight, [2017] | Series: Plants vs. zombies
Summary: When Zomboss's sun vacuum is blown up and scattered throughout time and space, Nate and Patrice race against the zombies to see who can gather all the missing pieces first.
Identifiers: LCCN 2016934738 | ISBN 9781614795438 (v.1 : lib. bdg.) | ISBN 9781614795445 (v.2 : lib. bdg.) | ISBN 9781614795452 (v.3 : lib. bdg.)
Subjects: LCSH: Time travel--Juvenile fiction. | Plants--Juvenile fiction. | Zombies--Juvenile fiction. | Adventure and adventurers--Juvenile fiction. | Comic books, strips, etc.--Juvenile fiction. | Graphic novels--Juvenile fiction.
Classification: DDC 741.5--dc23
LC record available at http://lccn.loc.gov/2016934738

Spotlight

A Division of ABDO
abdopublishing.com

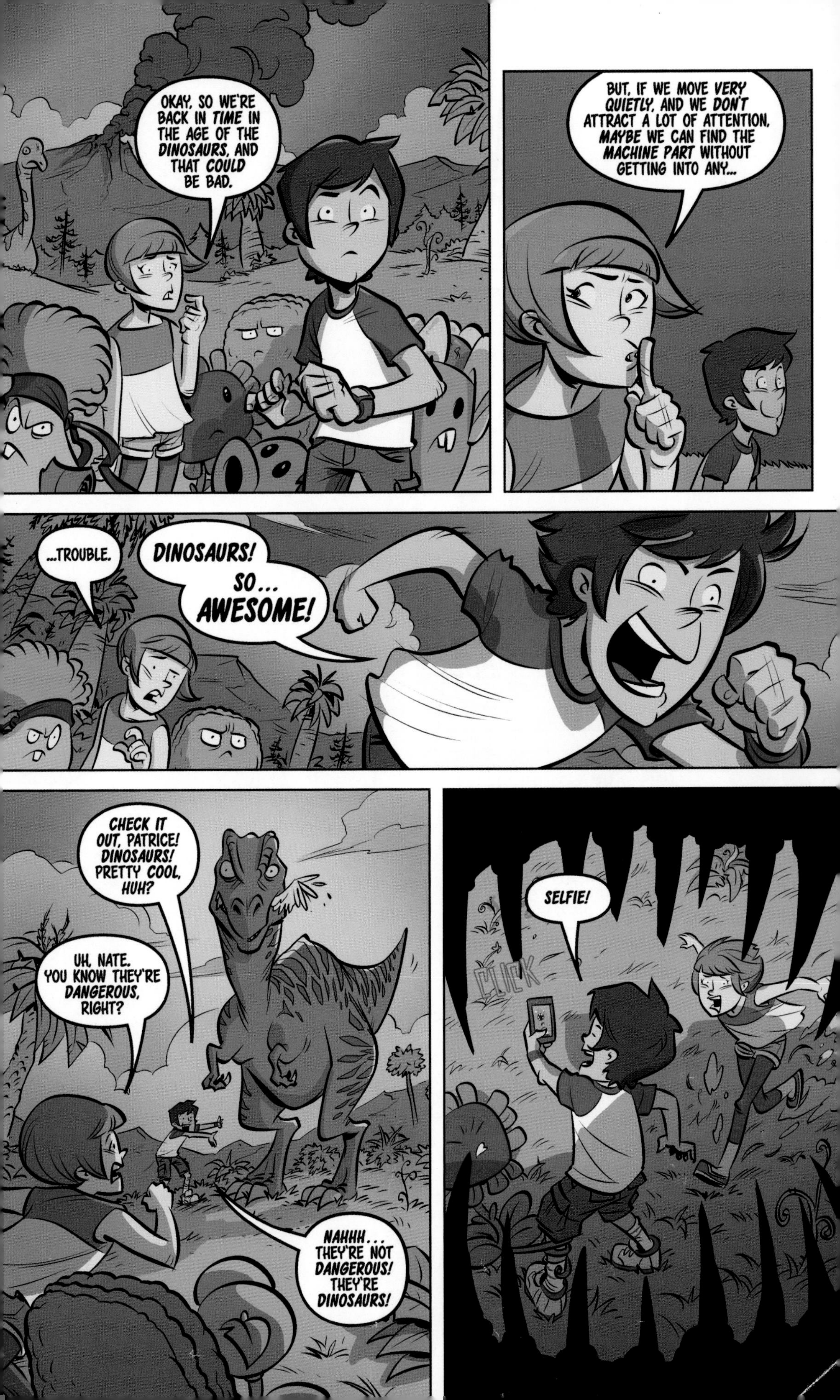

OKAY, SO WE'RE BACK IN TIME IN THE AGE OF THE DINOSAURS, AND THAT COULD BE BAD.
BUT, IF WE MOVE VERY QUIETLY, AND WE DON'T ATTRACT A LOT OF ATTENTION, MAYBE WE CAN FIND THE MACHINE PART WITHOUT GETTING INTO ANY...
...TROUBLE.
DINOSAURS! SO... AWESOME!
CHECK IT OUT, PATRICE! DINOSAURS! PRETTY COOL, HUH?
UH, NATE. YOU KNOW THEY'RE DANGEROUS, RIGHT?
NAHHH... THEY'RE NOT DANGEROUS! THEY'RE DINOSAURS!
SELFIE!
CLICK

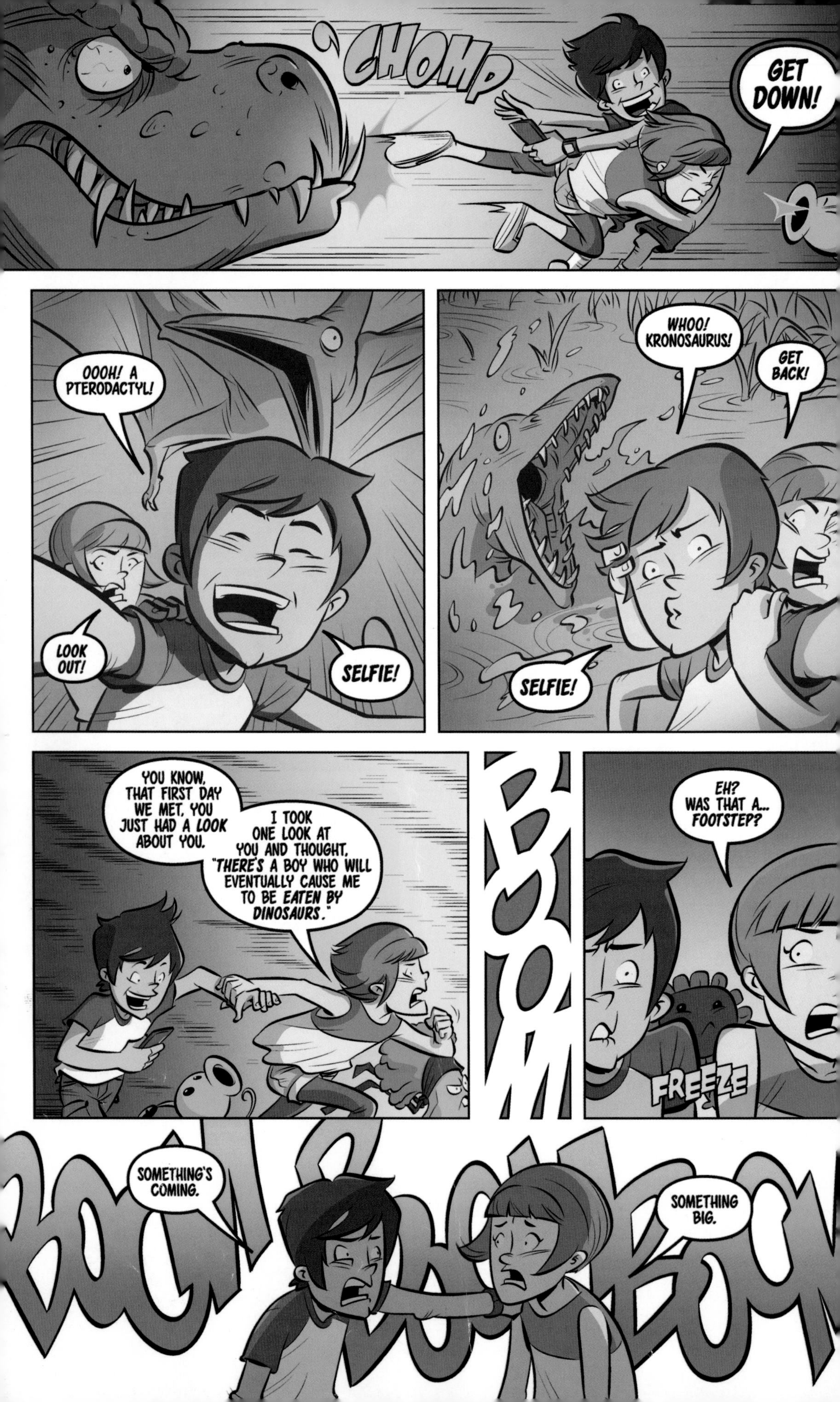
CHOMP
GET DOWN!
OOOH! A PTERODACTYL!
LOOK OUT!
SELFIE!
WHOO! KRONOSAURUS!
GET BACK!
SELFIE!
YOU KNOW, THAT FIRST DAY WE MET, YOU JUST HAD A *LOOK* ABOUT YOU.
I TOOK ONE LOOK AT YOU AND THOUGHT, "*THERE'S A BOY WHO WILL* EVENTUALLY CAUSE ME TO BE *EATEN BY DINOSAURS.*"
BOOM
EH? WAS THAT A... FOOTSTEP?
FREEZE
SOMETHING'S COMING.
SOMETHING BIG.

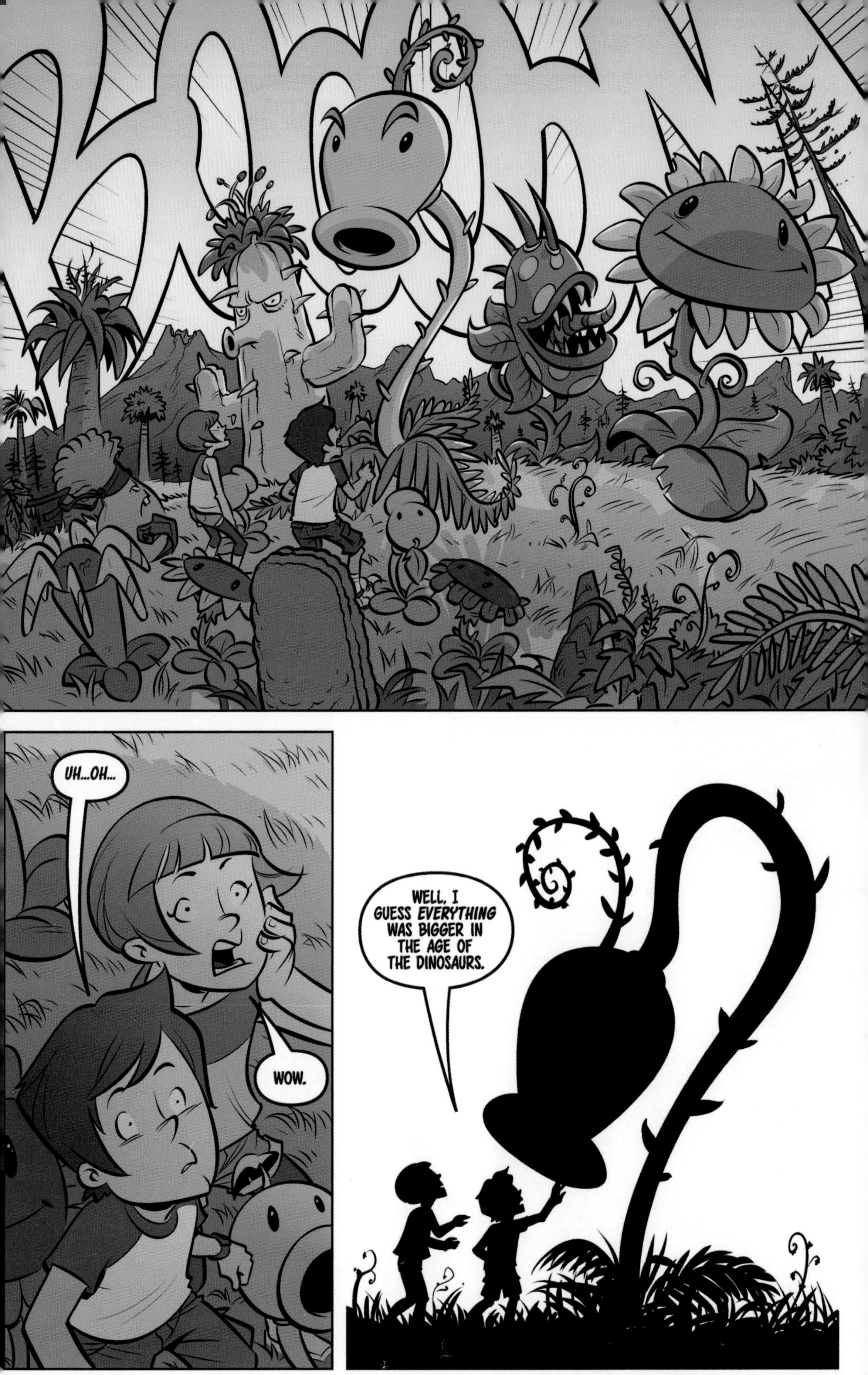
UH...OH...
WOW.
WELL, I GUESS *EVERYTHING* WAS BIGGER IN THE AGE OF THE DINOSAURS.

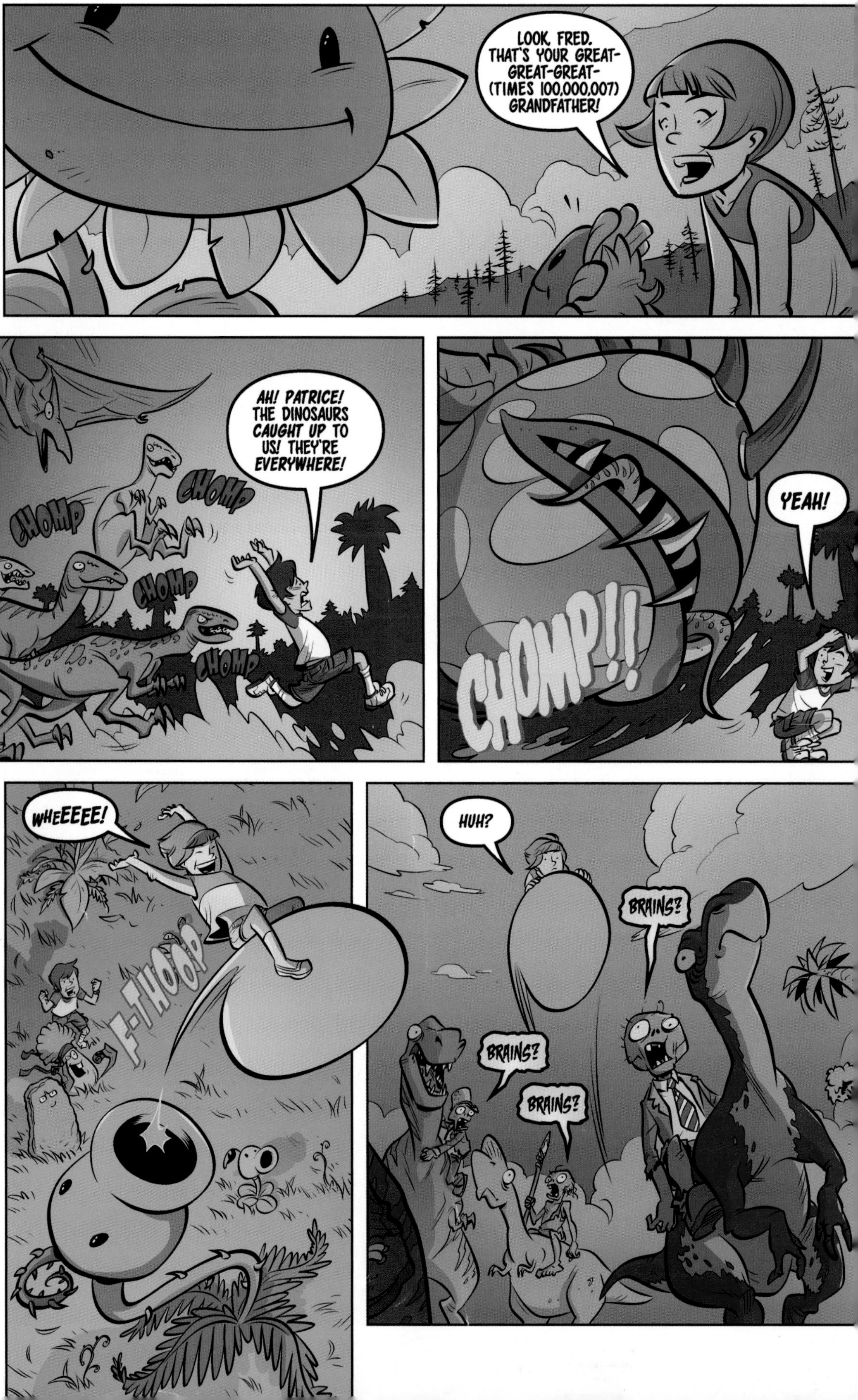

LOOK, FRED. THAT'S YOUR GREAT-GREAT-GREAT-(TIMES 100,000,007) GRANDFATHER!
AH! PATRICE! THE DINOSAURS CAUGHT UP TO US! THEY'RE EVERYWHERE!
CHOMP
CHOMP
CHOMP
CHOMP
YEAH!
CHOMP!!!
WHEEEEE!
F-THOOP
HUH?
BRAINS?
BRAINS?
BRAINS?

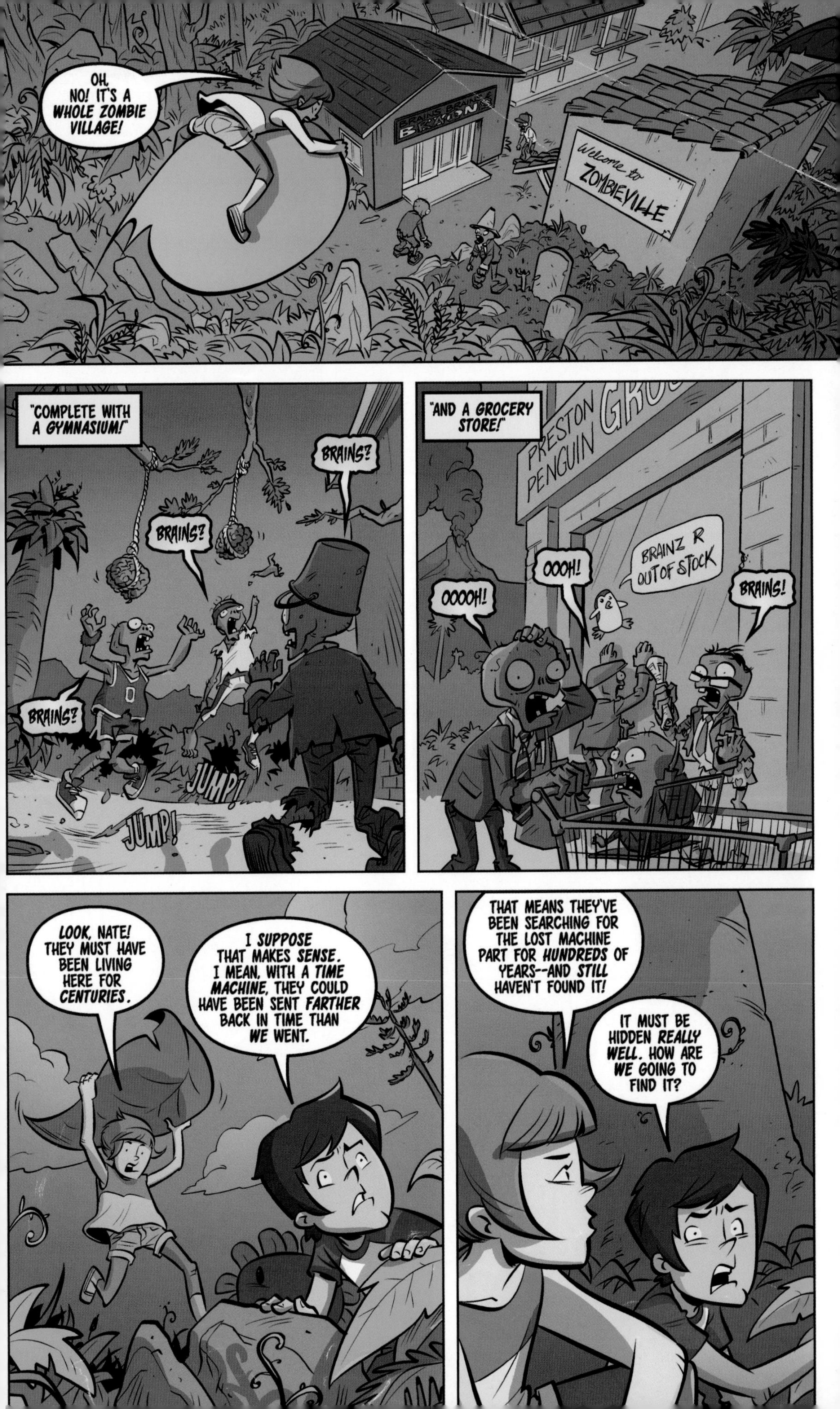
OH, NO! IT'S A WHOLE ZOMBIE VILLAGE!
Welcome to ZOMBIEVILLE
"COMPLETE WITH A GYMNASIUM!"
BRAINS?
BRAINS?
BRAINS?
JUMP!
JUMP!
"AND A GROCERY STORE!"
PRESTON PENGUIN
OOOOH!
OOOH!
BRAINZ R OUT OF STOCK
BRAINS!
LOOK, NATE! THEY MUST HAVE BEEN LIVING HERE FOR CENTURIES.
I SUPPOSE THAT MAKES SENSE. I MEAN, WITH A TIME MACHINE, THEY COULD HAVE BEEN SENT FARTHER BACK IN TIME THAN WE WENT.
THAT MEANS THEY'VE BEEN SEARCHING FOR THE LOST MACHINE PART FOR HUNDREDS OF YEARS--AND STILL HAVEN'T FOUND IT!
IT MUST BE HIDDEN REALLY WELL. HOW ARE WE GOING TO FIND IT?

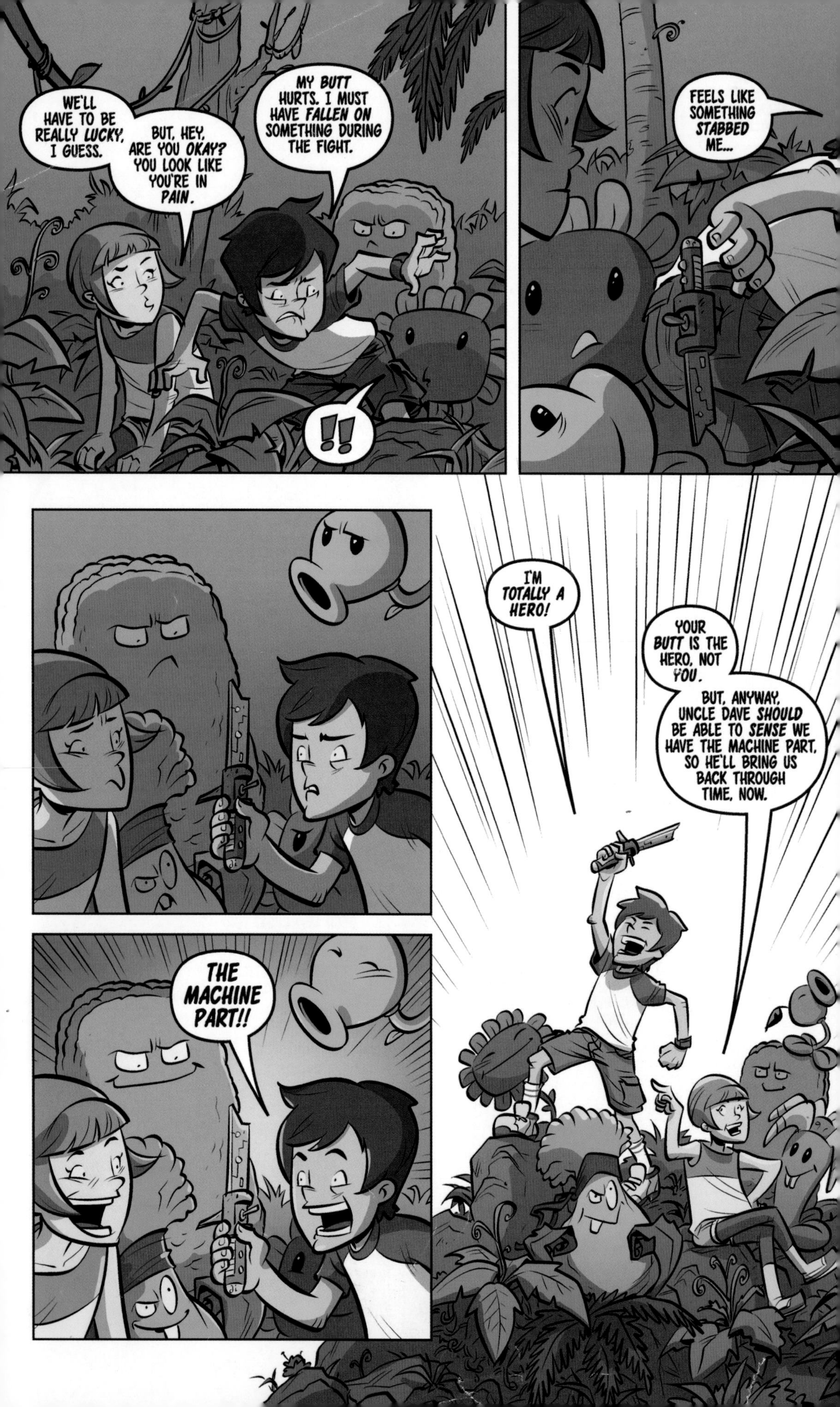

WE'LL HAVE TO BE REALLY LUCKY, I GUESS.
BUT, HEY, ARE YOU OKAY? YOU LOOK LIKE YOU'RE IN PAIN.
MY BUTT HURTS. I MUST HAVE FALLEN ON SOMETHING DURING THE FIGHT.
!!
FEELS LIKE SOMETHING STABBED ME...
THE MACHINE PART!!
I'M TOTALLY A HERO!
YOUR BUTT IS THE HERO, NOT YOU.
BUT, ANYWAY, UNCLE DAVE SHOULD BE ABLE TO SENSE WE HAVE THE MACHINE PART, SO HE'LL BRING US BACK THROUGH TIME, NOW.

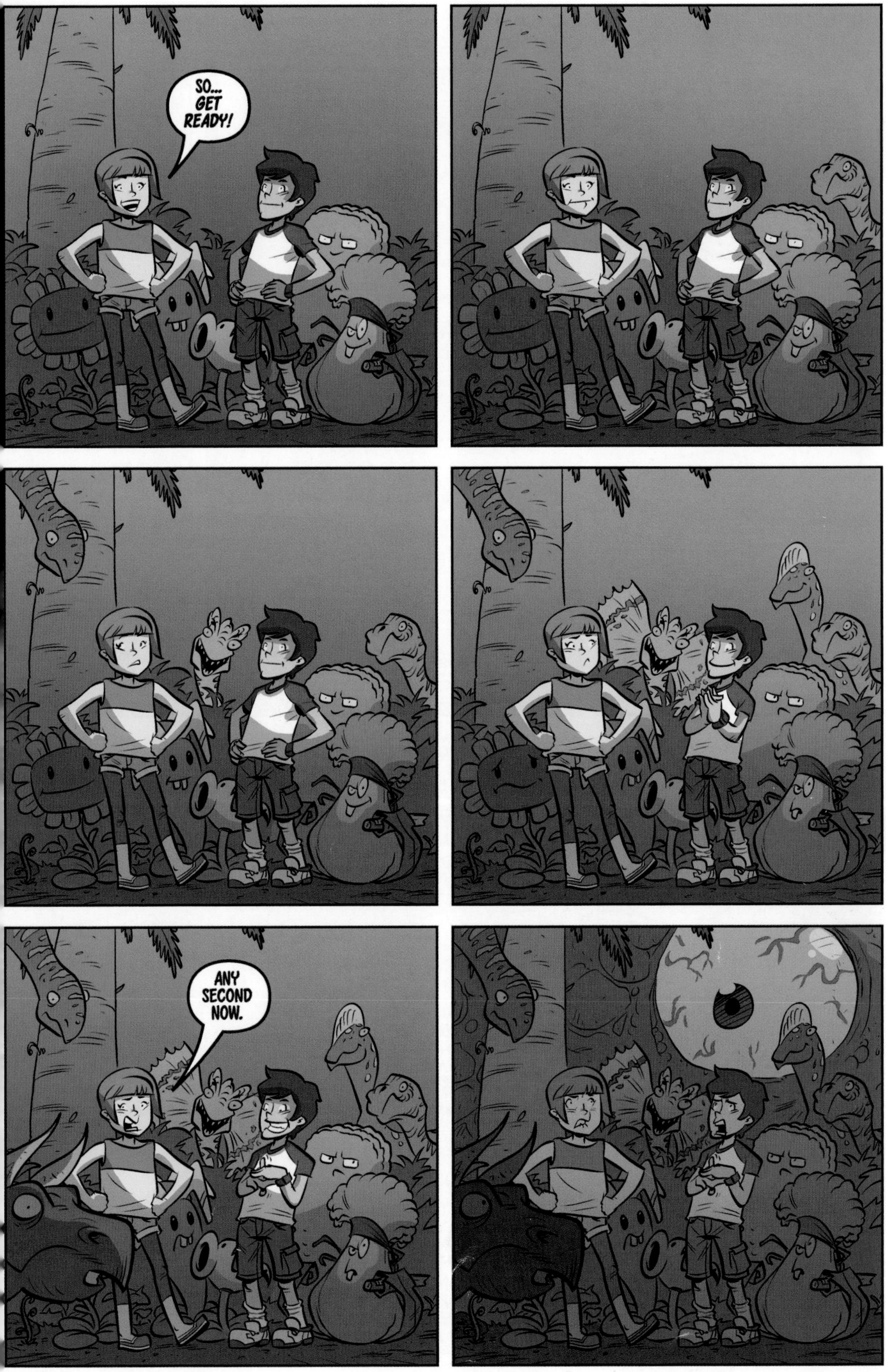
SO... GET READY!
ANY SECOND NOW.

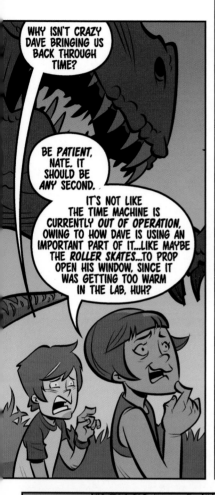

WHY ISN'T CRAZY DAVE BRINGING US BACK THROUGH TIME?

BE PATIENT, NATE. IT SHOULD BE ANY SECOND.

IT'S NOT LIKE THE TIME MACHINE IS CURRENTLY *OUT OF OPERATION*, OWING TO HOW DAVE IS USING AN IMPORTANT PART OF IT...LIKE MAYBE THE *ROLLER SKATES*...TO PROP OPEN HIS WINDOW, SINCE IT WAS GETTING TOO WARM IN THE LAB, HUH?

MEANWHILE, MILLIONS OF YEARS IN THE FUTURE...

LA, LA, LA! GARBLE-GRABBLE LA!

OH, THAT'S *TOTALLY* HAPPENING.

OKAY, SO YOU AND I HAVE TO SURVIVE *LONG ENOUGH* FOR DAVE TO REMEMBER THAT HE SENT US BACK TO THE *AGE OF THE DINOSAURS* IN AN ATTEMPT TO SAVE THE WORLD.

YOU KNOW, THAT'S SOMETHING THAT *MOST OF US*, QUITE FRANKLY, WOULD *REMEMBER*.

WELL, WE NEED TO REMEMBER TO *FIGHT*!

FIGHT? I THOUGHT WE WERE GOING TO *RUN*.

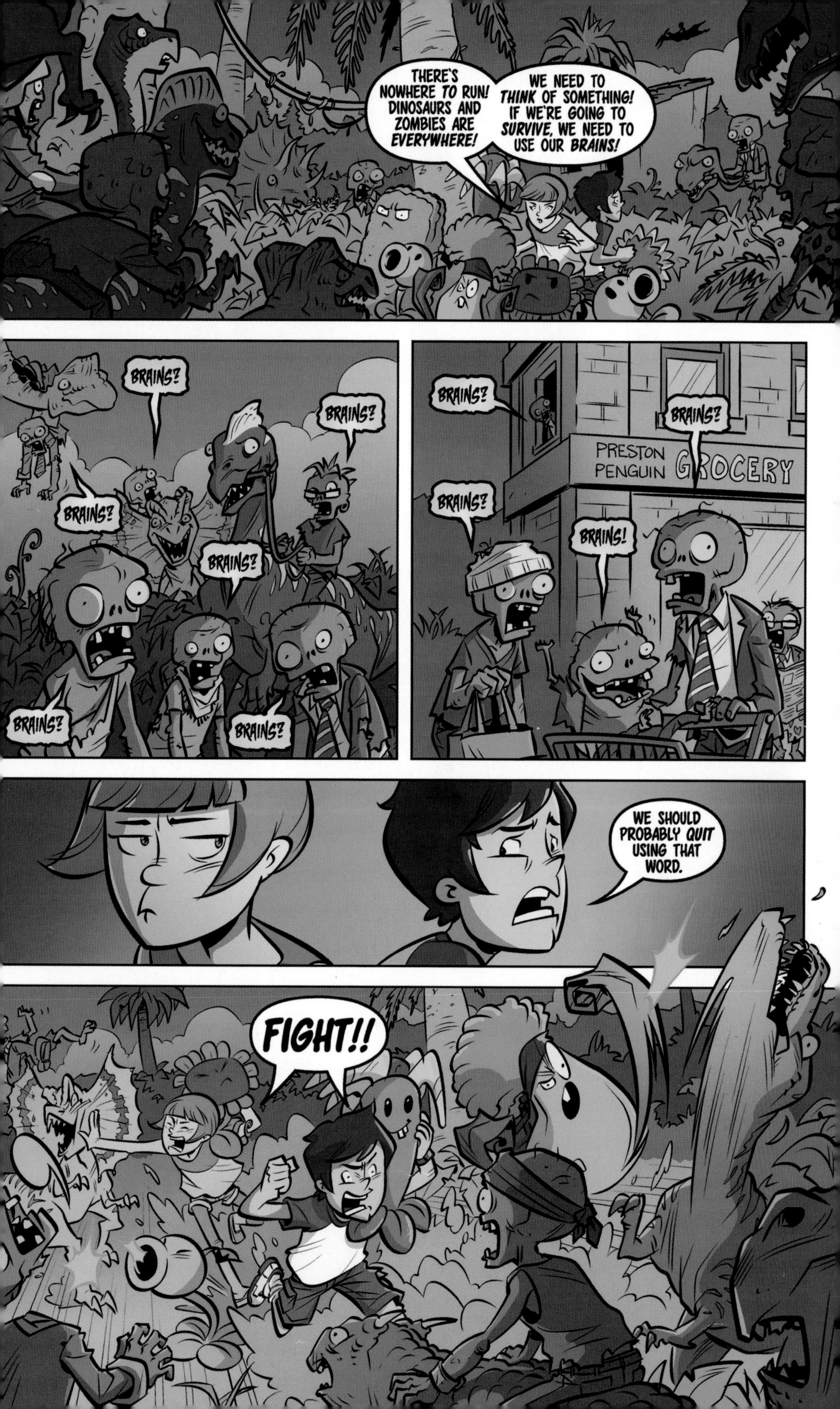
THERE'S NOWHERE TO RUN! DINOSAURS AND ZOMBIES ARE EVERYWHERE!
WE NEED TO THINK OF SOMETHING! IF WE'RE GOING TO SURVIVE, WE NEED TO USE OUR BRAINS!
BRAINS?
BRAINS?
BRAINS?
BRAINS?
BRAINS?
BRAINS?
BRAINS?
BRAINS?
PRESTON PENGUIN GROCERY
BRAINS?
BRAINS!
WE SHOULD PROBABLY QUIT USING THAT WORD.
FIGHT!!

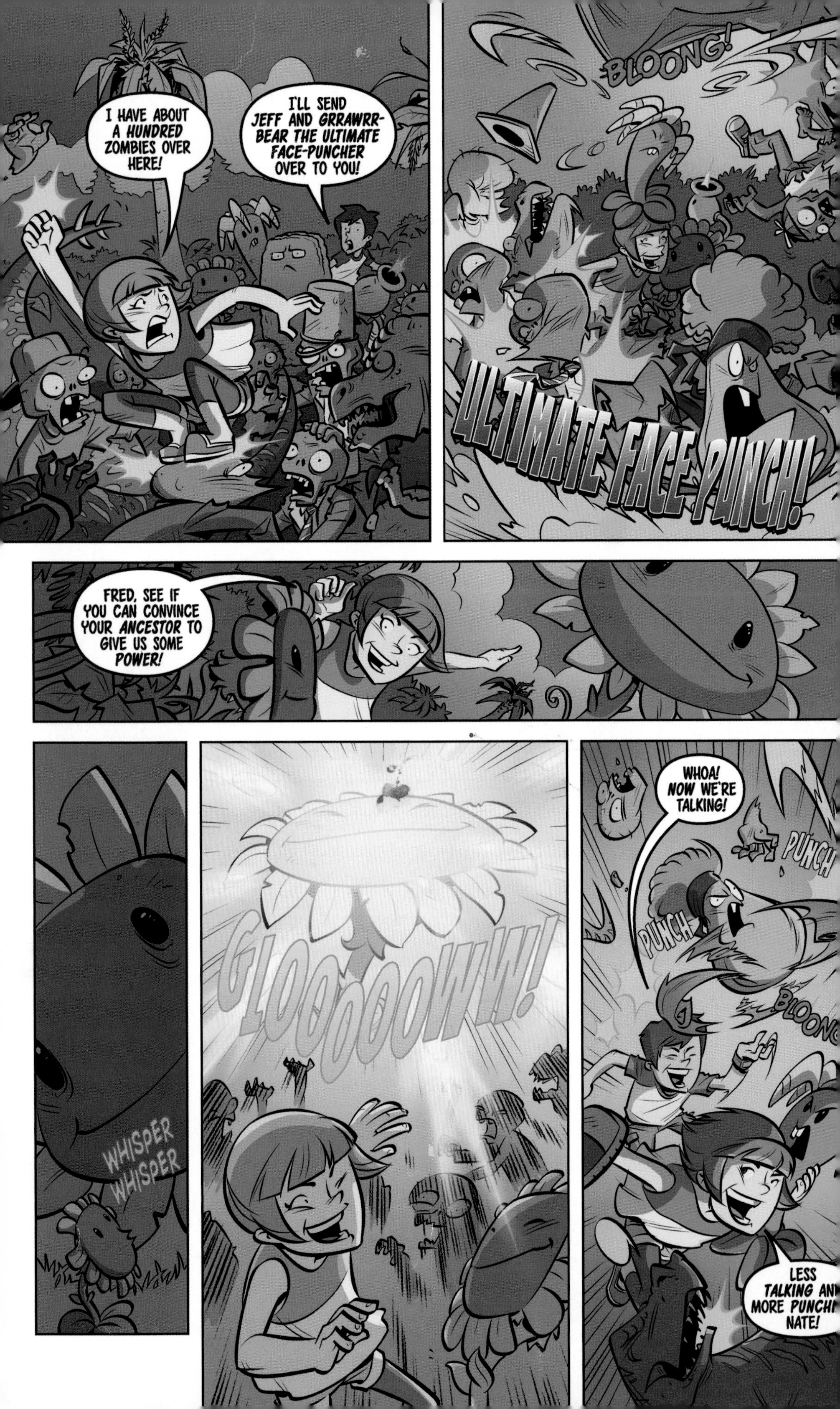
I HAVE ABOUT A *HUNDRED* ZOMBIES OVER HERE!
I'LL SEND *JEFF* AND *GRRAWRR-BEAR THE ULTIMATE FACE-PUNCHER* OVER TO YOU!
BLOONG!
ULTIMATE FACE PUNCH!
FRED, SEE IF YOU CAN CONVINCE YOUR *ANCESTOR* TO GIVE US SOME *POWER!*
WHISPER WHISPER
GLOOOOOWW!
WHOA! *NOW* WE'RE TALKING!
PUNCH
PUNCH
BLOONG
LESS *TALKING* AN
MORE *PUNCHI*
NATE!

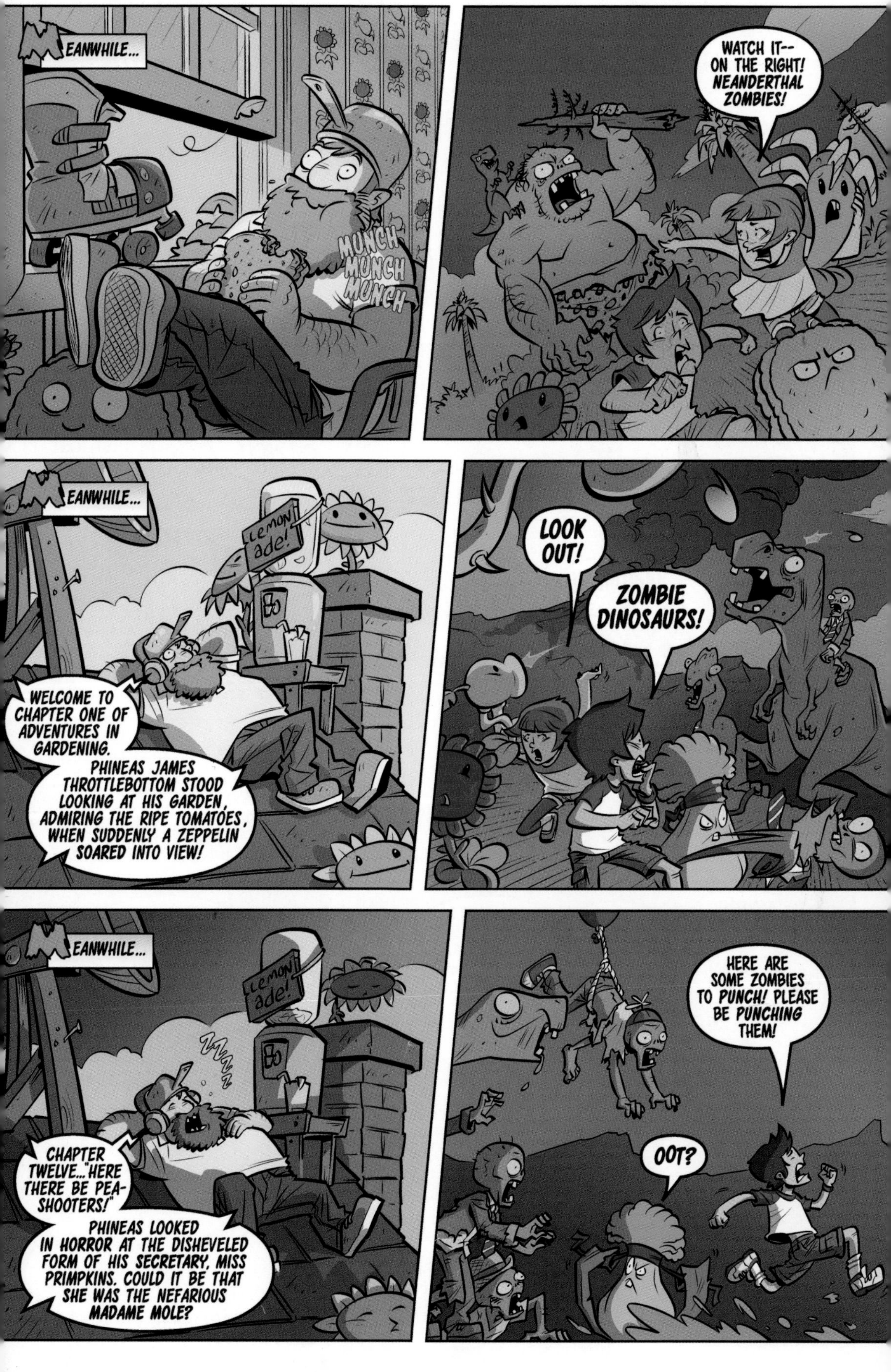
MEANWHILE...
MUNCH MUNCH MUNCH
WATCH IT-- ON THE RIGHT! NEANDERTHAL ZOMBIES!
MEANWHILE...
LEMON ade!
WELCOME TO CHAPTER ONE OF ADVENTURES IN GARDENING.
PHINEAS JAMES THROTTLEBOTTOM STOOD LOOKING AT HIS GARDEN, ADMIRING THE RIPE TOMATOES, WHEN SUDDENLY A ZEPPELIN SOARED INTO VIEW!
LOOK OUT!
ZOMBIE DINOSAURS!
MEANWHILE...
LEMON ade!
ZZZ
CHAPTER TWELVE..."HERE THERE BE PEA-SHOOTERS!"
PHINEAS LOOKED IN HORROR AT THE DISHEVELED FORM OF HIS SECRETARY, MISS PRIMPKINS. COULD IT BE THAT SHE WAS THE NEFARIOUS MADAME MOLE?
HERE ARE SOME ZOMBIES TO PUNCH! PLEASE BE PUNCHING THEM!
OOT?

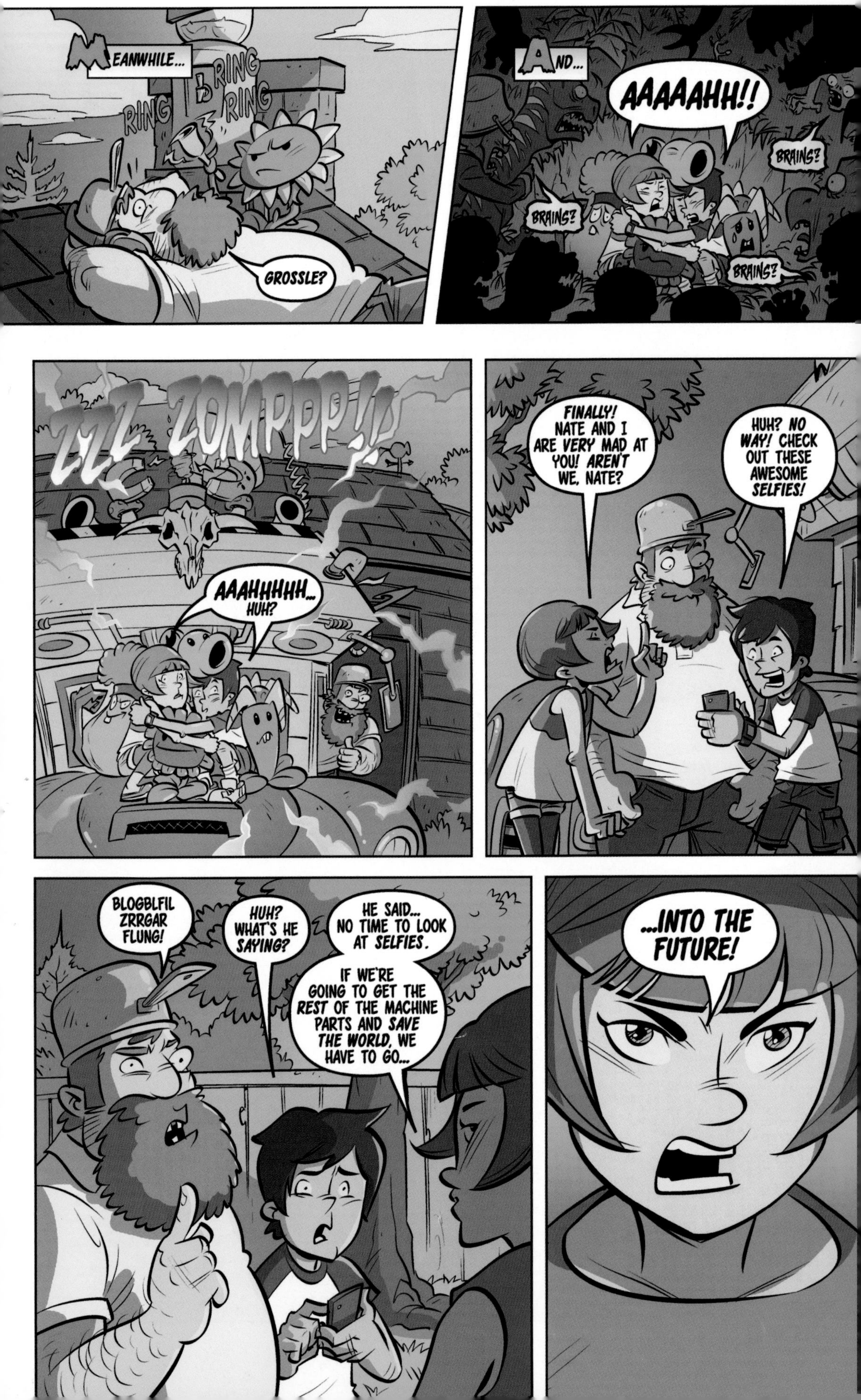
MEANWHILE...
RING RING RING
GROSSLE?
AND...
AAAAAHH!!
BRAINS?
BRAINS?
BRAINS?
ZZZ ZOMPPP!!!
AAAHHHHH... HUH?
FINALLY! NATE AND I ARE VERY MAD AT YOU! AREN'T WE, NATE?
HUH? NO WAY! CHECK OUT THESE AWESOME SELFIES!
BLOGBLFIL ZRRGAR FLUNG!
HUH? WHAT'S HE SAYING?
HE SAID... NO TIME TO LOOK AT SELFIES.
IF WE'RE GOING TO GET THE REST OF THE MACHINE PARTS AND SAVE THE WORLD, WE HAVE TO GO...
...INTO THE FUTURE!

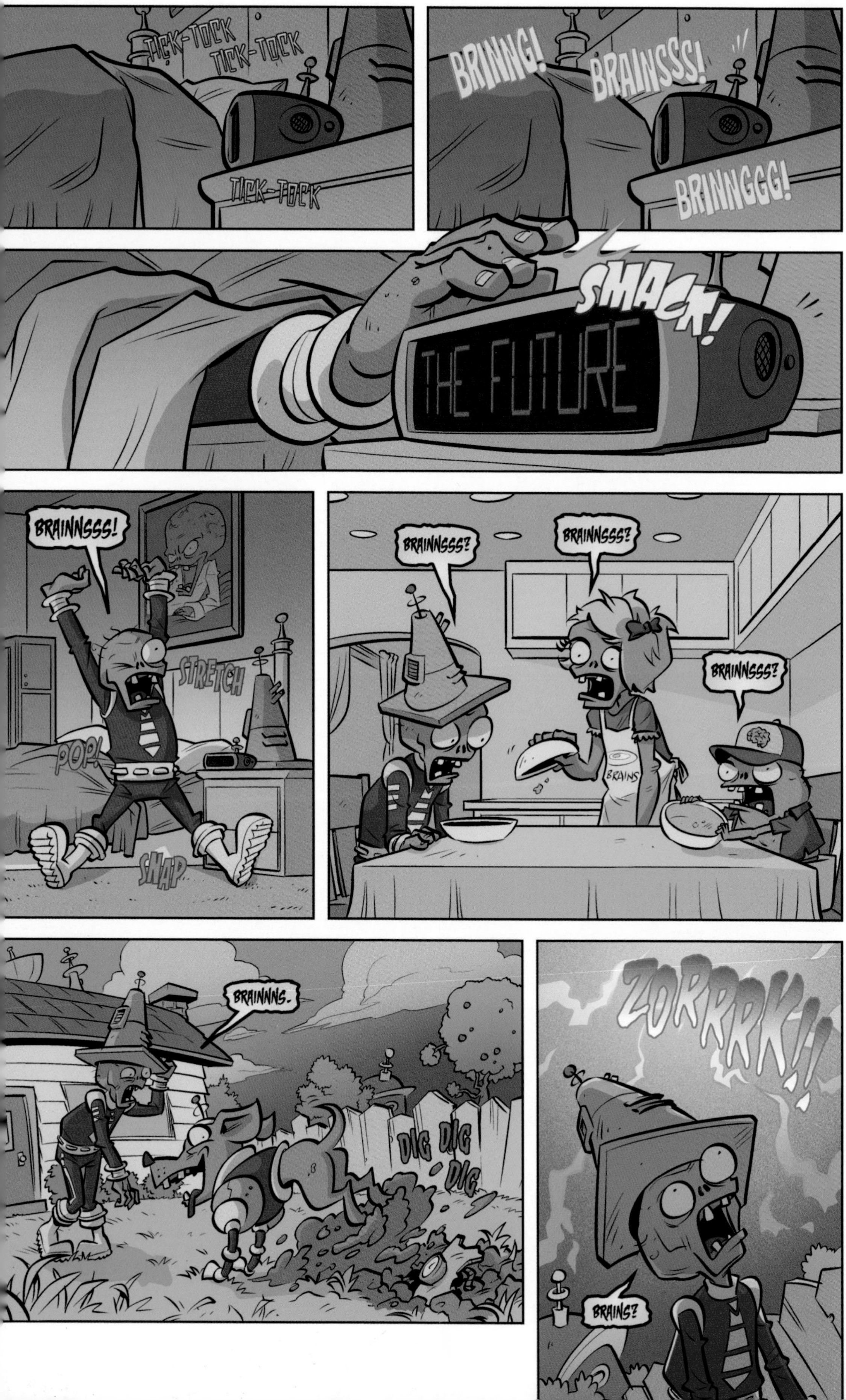
TICK-TOCK
TICK-TOCK
TICK-TOCK
BRINNG!
BRAINSSS!
BRINNGGG!
SMACK!
THE FUTURE
BRAINNSSS!
STRETCH
POP!
SNAP
BRAINNSSS?
BRAINNSSS?
BRAINNSSS?
BRAINS
BRAINNNS.
DIG DIG
DIG
ZORRRK!!
BRAINS?

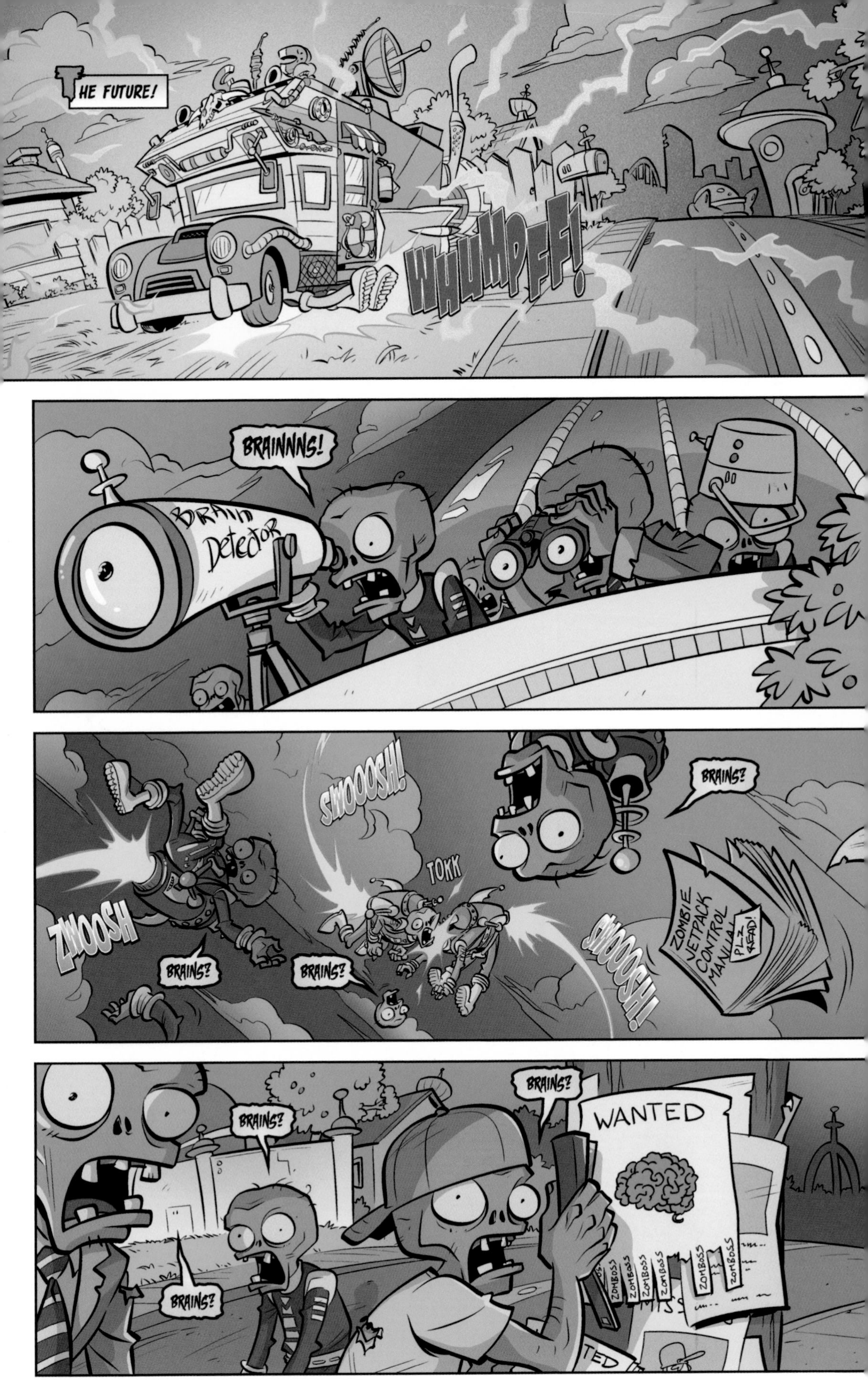
THE FUTURE!
WHUMPFF!
BRAINNNS!
BRAIN Detector
SWOOOSH!
BRAINS?
TOKK
ZWOOSH
BRAINS?
BRAINS?
SWOOOSH!
ZOMBIE JETPACK CONTROL MANUAL
PLZ READ!
BRAINS?
BRAINS?
BRAINS?
WANTED
ZOMBOSS
ZOMBOSS
ZOMBOSS
ZOMBOSS
ZOMBOSS
ZOMBOSS
ZOMBOSS

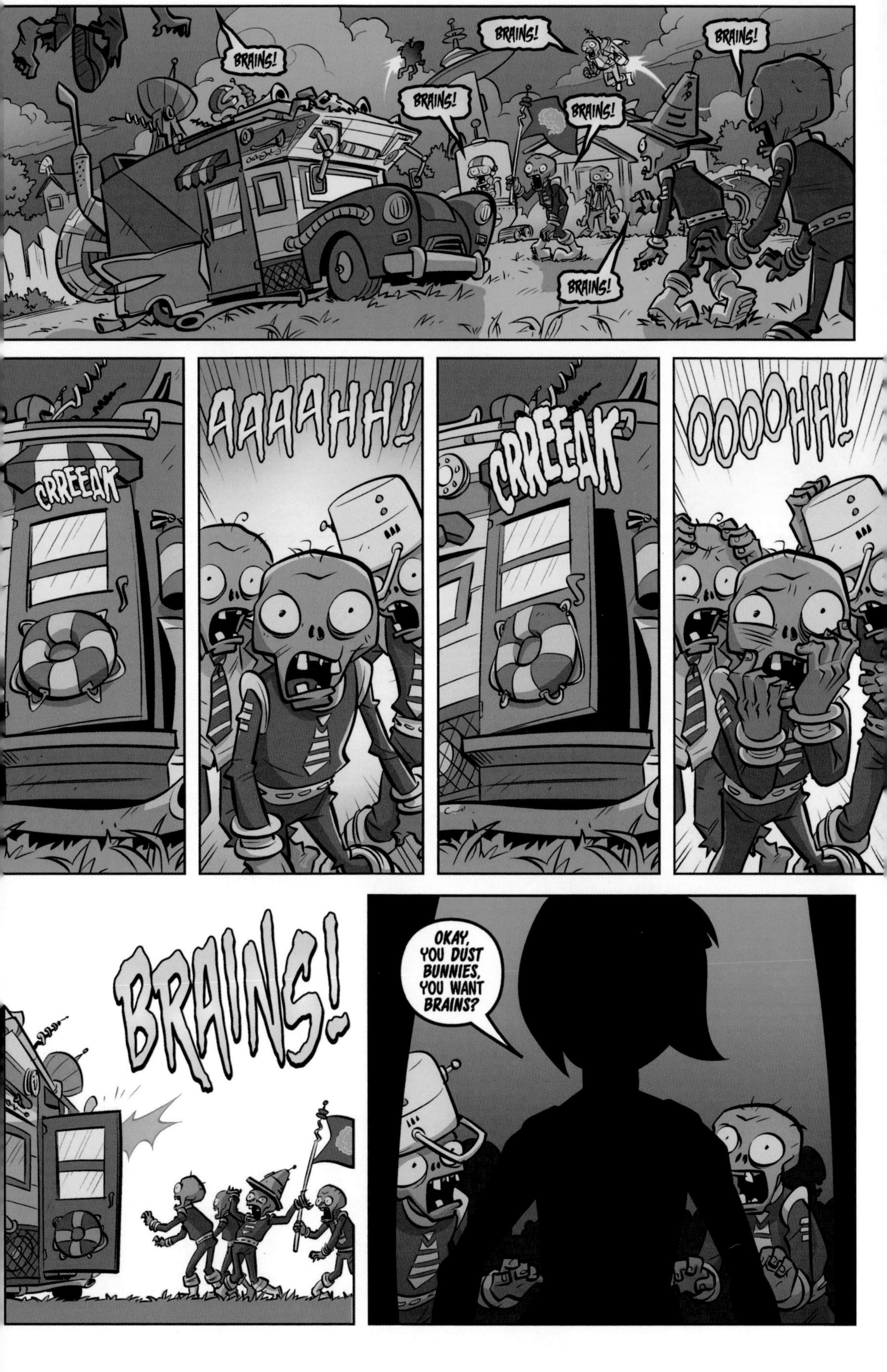
BRAINS!
BRAINS!
BRAINS!
BRAINS!
BRAINS!
BRAINS!
BRAINS!
CRREEAK
AAAAHH!
CRREEAK
OOOOHH!
BRAINS!
OKAY, YOU DUST BUNNIES, YOU WANT BRAINS?

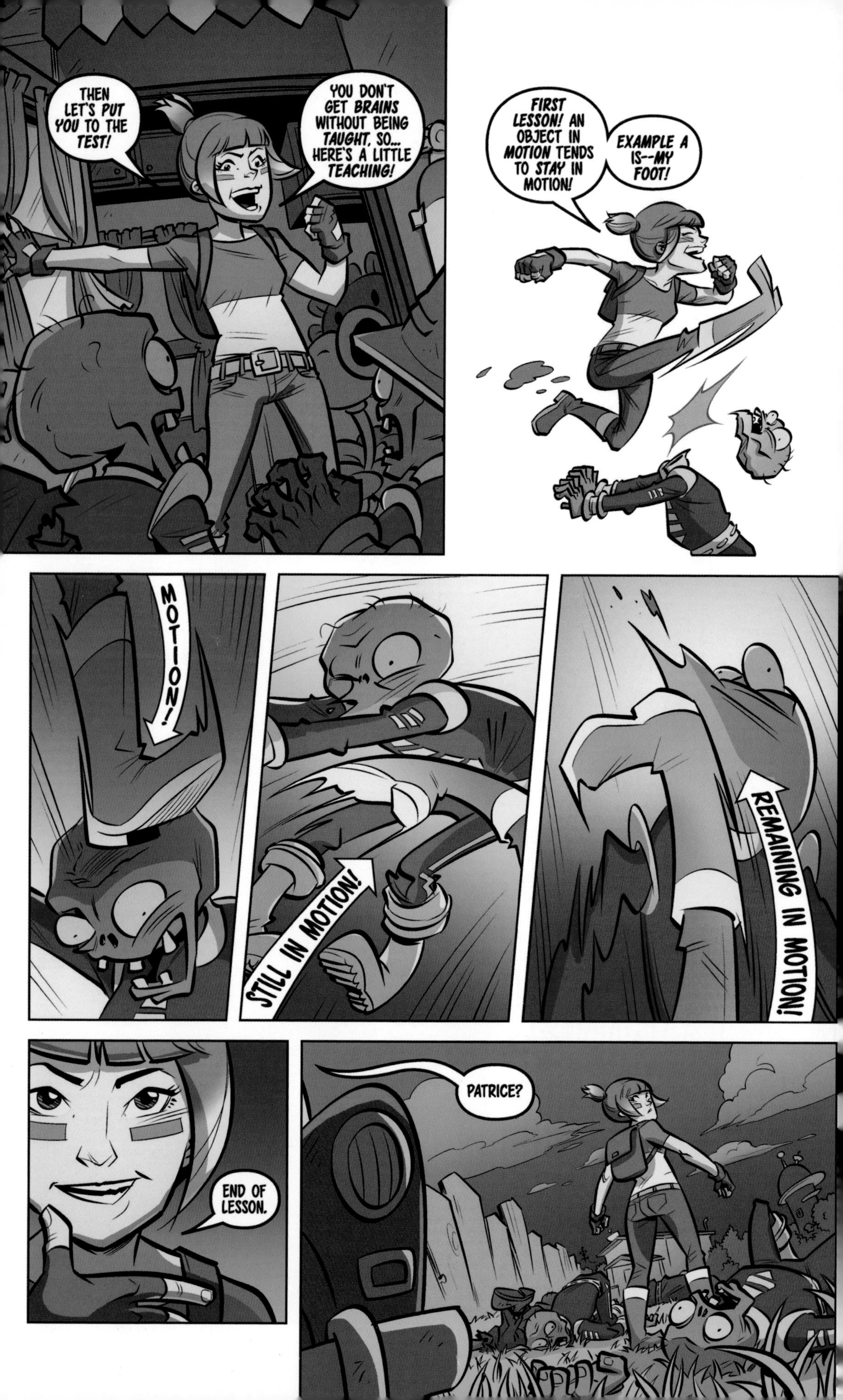
THEN LET'S PUT YOU TO THE TEST!
YOU DON'T GET BRAINS WITHOUT BEING TAUGHT, SO... HERE'S A LITTLE TEACHING!
FIRST LESSON! AN OBJECT IN MOTION TENDS TO STAY IN MOTION!
EXAMPLE A IS--MY FOOT!
MOTION!
STILL IN MOTION!
REMAINING IN MOTION!
END OF LESSON.
PATRICE?

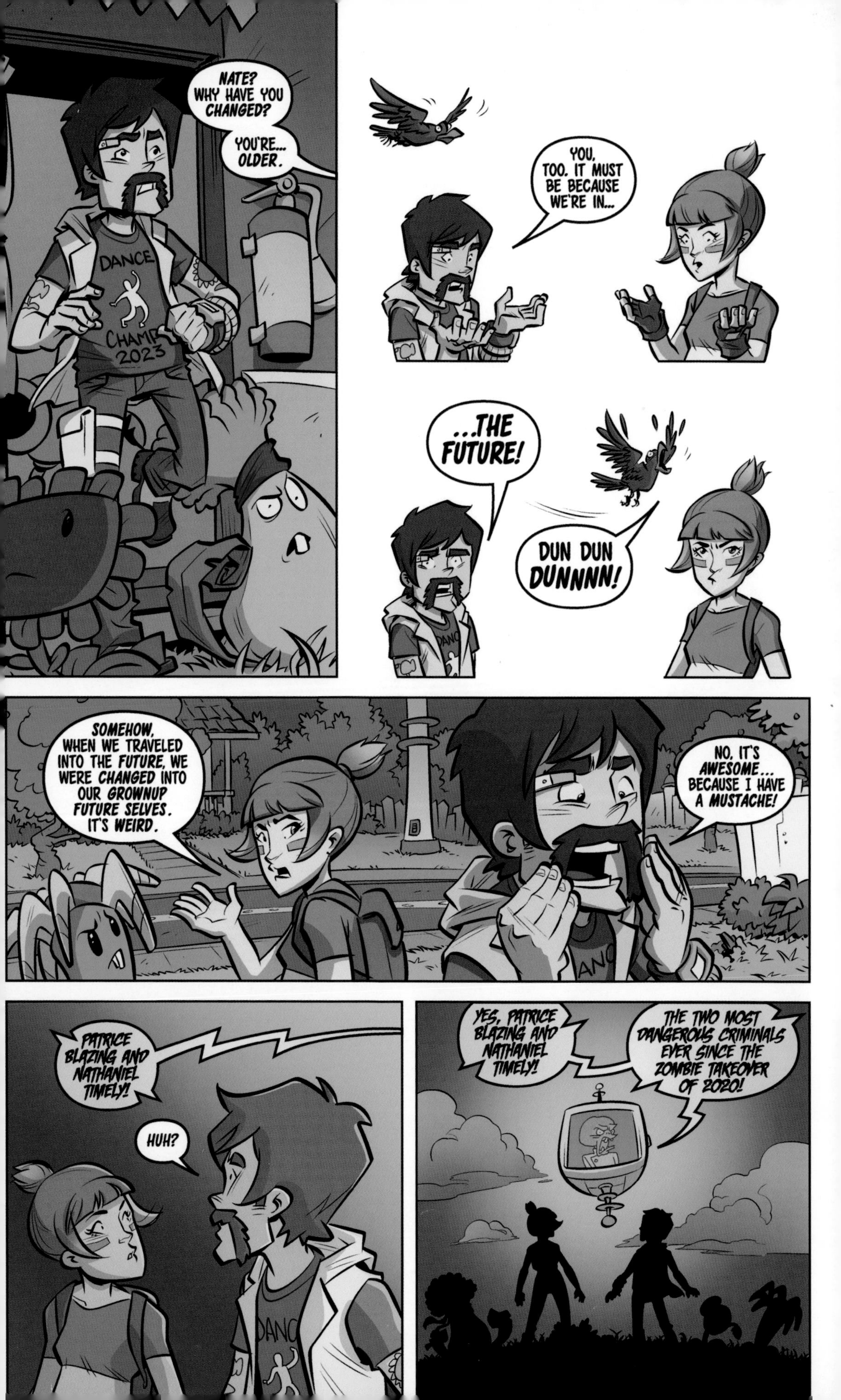
NATE? WHY HAVE YOU CHANGED?
YOU'RE... OLDER.
DANCE CHAMP 2023
YOU, TOO. IT MUST BE BECAUSE WE'RE IN...
...THE FUTURE!
DUN DUN DUNNNN!
SOMEHOW, WHEN WE TRAVELED INTO THE FUTURE, WE WERE CHANGED INTO OUR GROWNUP FUTURE SELVES. IT'S WEIRD.
NO, IT'S AWESOME... BECAUSE I HAVE A MUSTACHE!
PATRICE BLAZING AND NATHANIEL TIMELY!
HUH?
YES, PATRICE BLAZING AND NATHANIEL TIMELY!
THE TWO MOST DANGEROUS CRIMINALS EVER SINCE THE ZOMBIE TAKEOVER OF 2020!

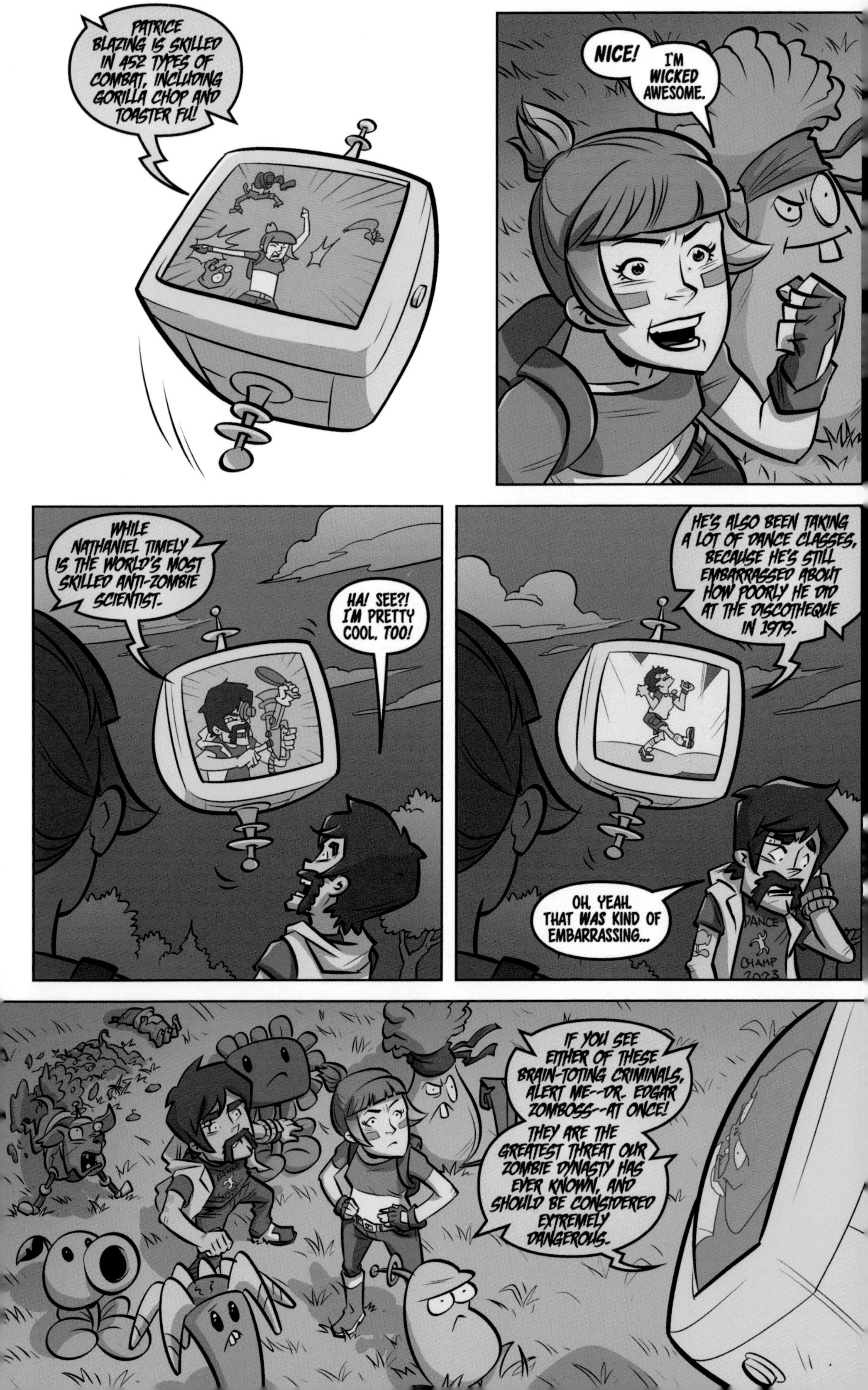
PATRICE BLAZING IS SKILLED IN 452 TYPES OF COMBAT, INCLUDING GORILLA CHOP AND TOASTER FU!
NICE!
I'M WICKED AWESOME.
WHILE NATHANIEL TIMELY IS THE WORLD'S MOST SKILLED ANTI-ZOMBIE SCIENTIST.
HA! SEE?! I'M PRETTY COOL, TOO!
HE'S ALSO BEEN TAKING A LOT OF DANCE CLASSES, BECAUSE HE'S STILL EMBARRASSED ABOUT HOW POORLY HE DID AT THE DISCOTHEQUE IN 1979.
OH, YEAH. THAT WAS KIND OF EMBARRASSING...
DANCE CHAMP 2023
IF YOU SEE EITHER OF THESE BRAIN-TOTING CRIMINALS, ALERT ME--DR. EDGAR ZOMBOSS--AT ONCE!
THEY ARE THE GREATEST THREAT OUR ZOMBIE DYNASTY HAS EVER KNOWN, AND SHOULD BE CONSIDERED EXTREMELY DANGEROUS.

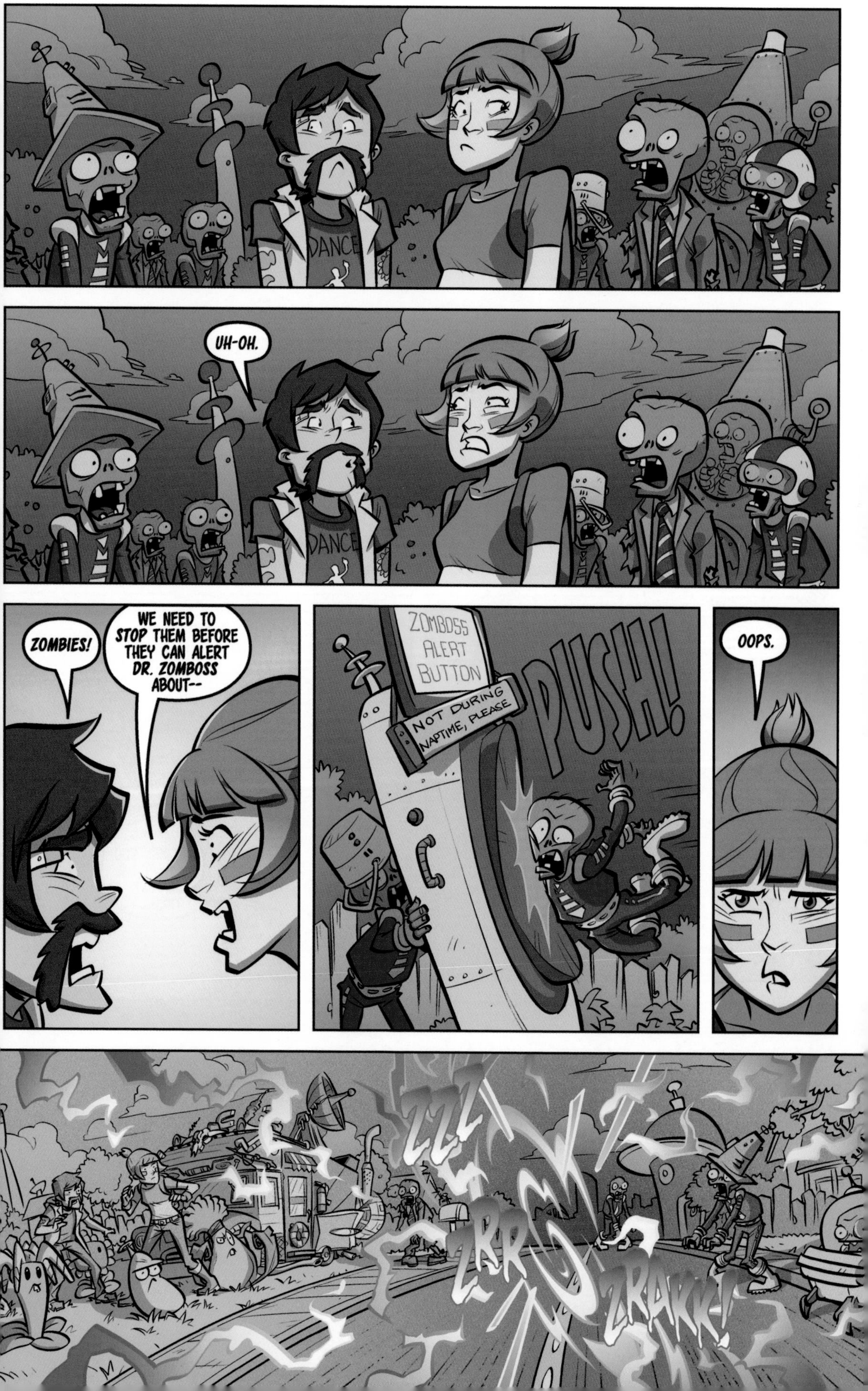
UH-OH.
ZOMBIES!
WE NEED TO STOP THEM BEFORE THEY CAN ALERT DR. ZOMBOSS ABOUT--
ZOMBOSS ALERT BUTTON
NOT DURING NAPTIME, PLEASE
PUSH!
OOPS.
ZZZ
ZRR
ZRAKK!

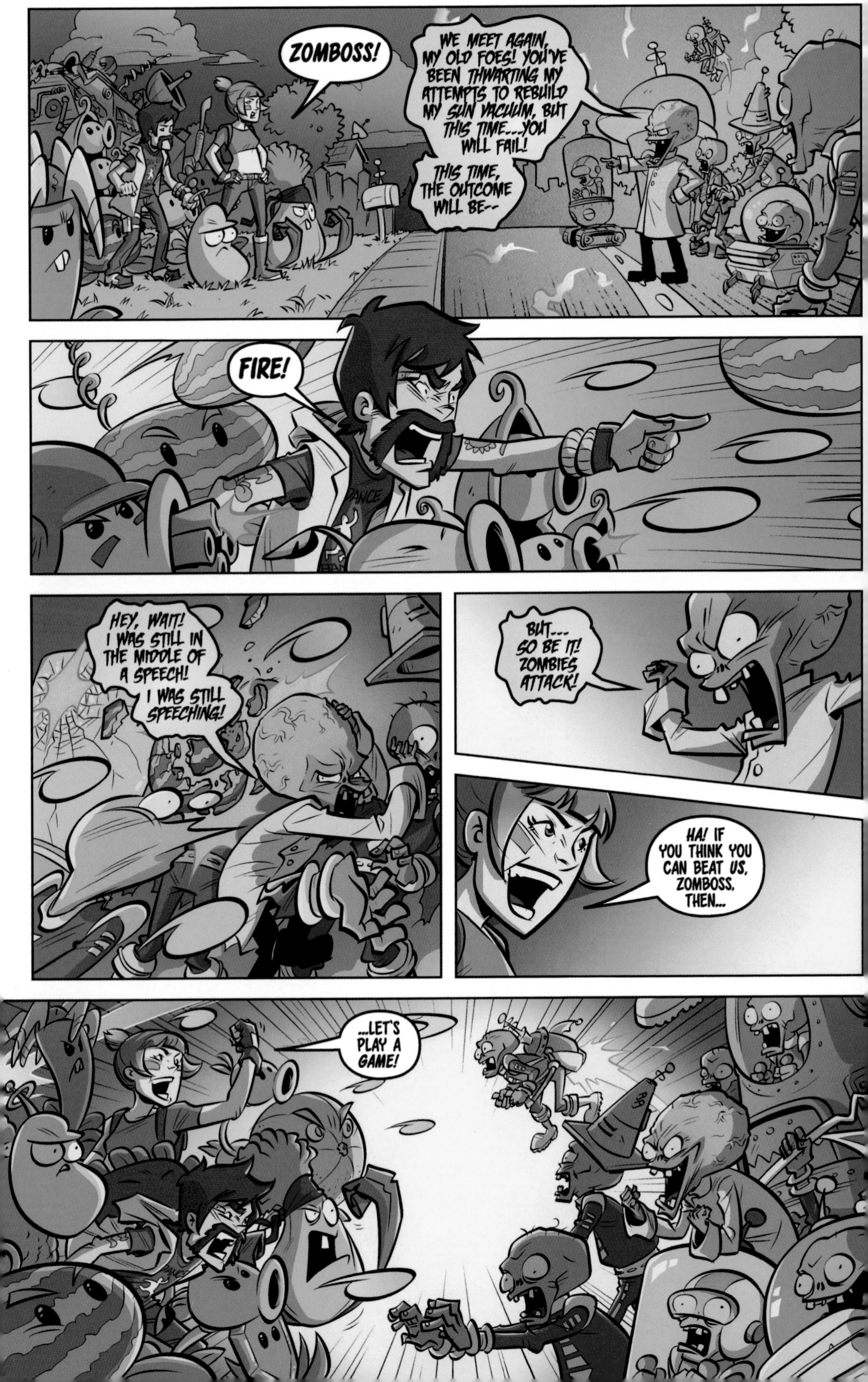
ZOMBOSS!
WE MEET AGAIN, MY OLD FOES! YOU'VE BEEN THWARTING MY ATTEMPTS TO REBUILD MY SUN VACUUM, BUT THIS TIME...YOU WILL FAIL!
THIS TIME, THE OUTCOME WILL BE--
FIRE!
HEY, WAIT! I WAS STILL IN THE MIDDLE OF A SPEECH!
I WAS STILL SPEECHING!
BUT... SO BE IT! ZOMBIES ATTACK!
HA! IF YOU THINK YOU CAN BEAT US, ZOMBOSS, THEN...
...LET'S PLAY A GAME!

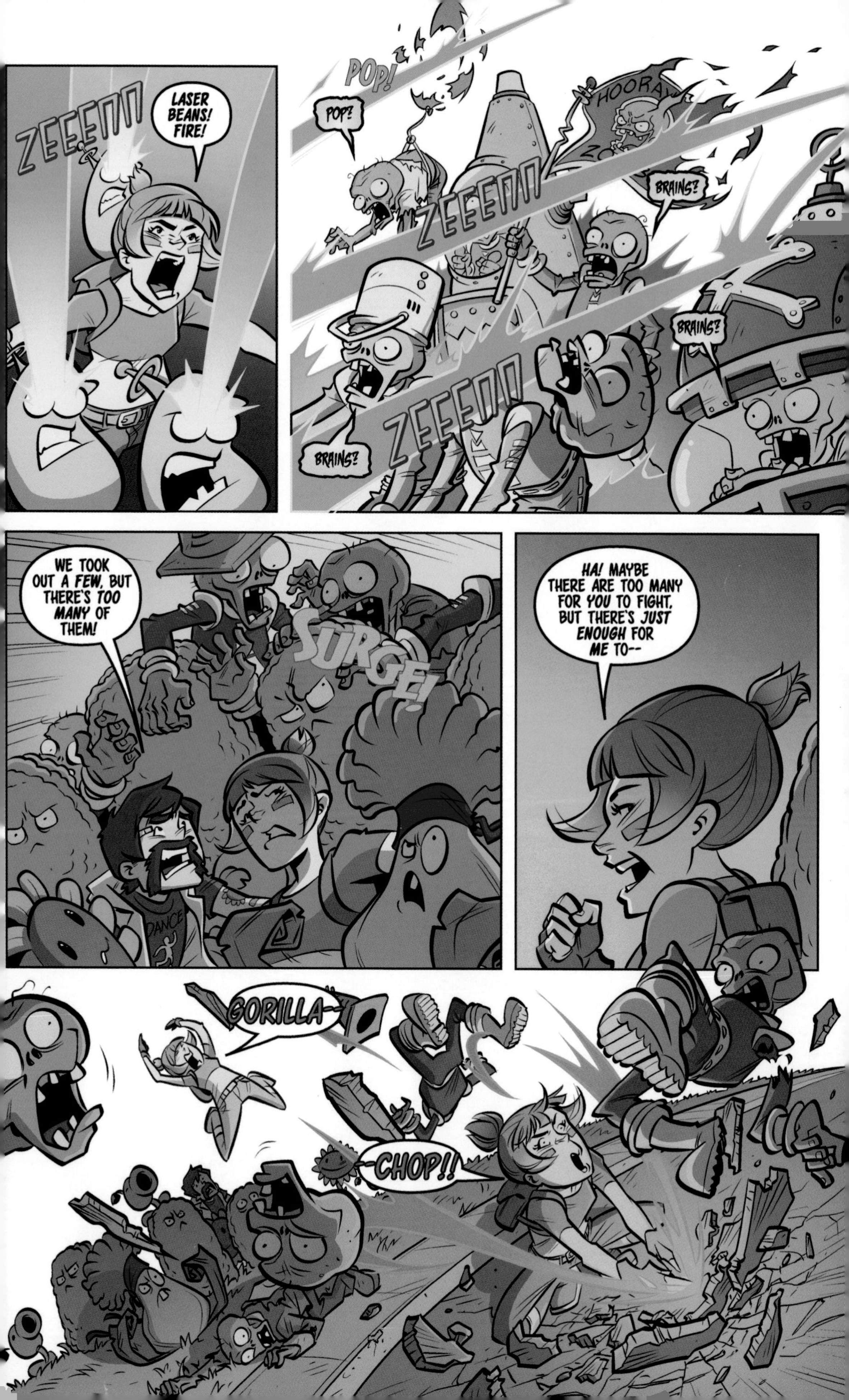
ZEEENN
LASER BEANS! FIRE!
POP!
POP?
ZEEENN
BRAINS?
BRAINS?
ZEEENN
BRAINS?
WE TOOK OUT A *FEW*, BUT THERE'S *TOO MANY* OF THEM!
SURGE!
HA! MAYBE THERE ARE TOO MANY FOR *YOU* TO FIGHT, BUT THERE'S *JUST ENOUGH* FOR *ME* TO--
GORILLA-
-CHOP!!

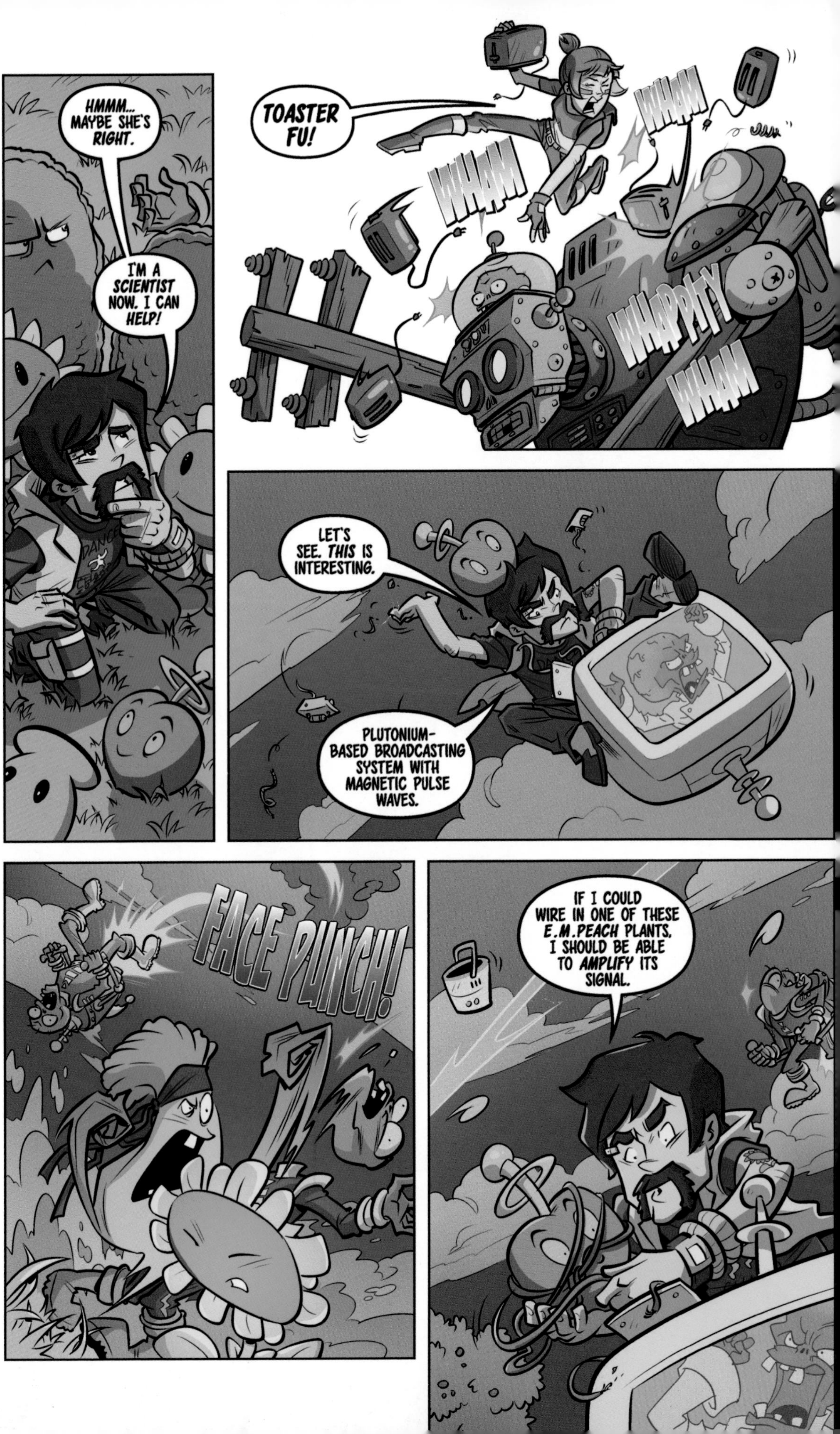
HMMM... MAYBE SHE'S RIGHT.
I'M A SCIENTIST NOW. I CAN HELP!
TOASTER FU!
WHAM
WHAM
WHAPPITY
WHAM
LET'S SEE. THIS IS INTERESTING.
PLUTONIUM-BASED BROADCASTING SYSTEM WITH MAGNETIC PULSE WAVES.
FACE PUNCH!
IF I COULD WIRE IN ONE OF THESE E.M.PEACH PLANTS, I SHOULD BE ABLE TO AMPLIFY ITS SIGNAL.

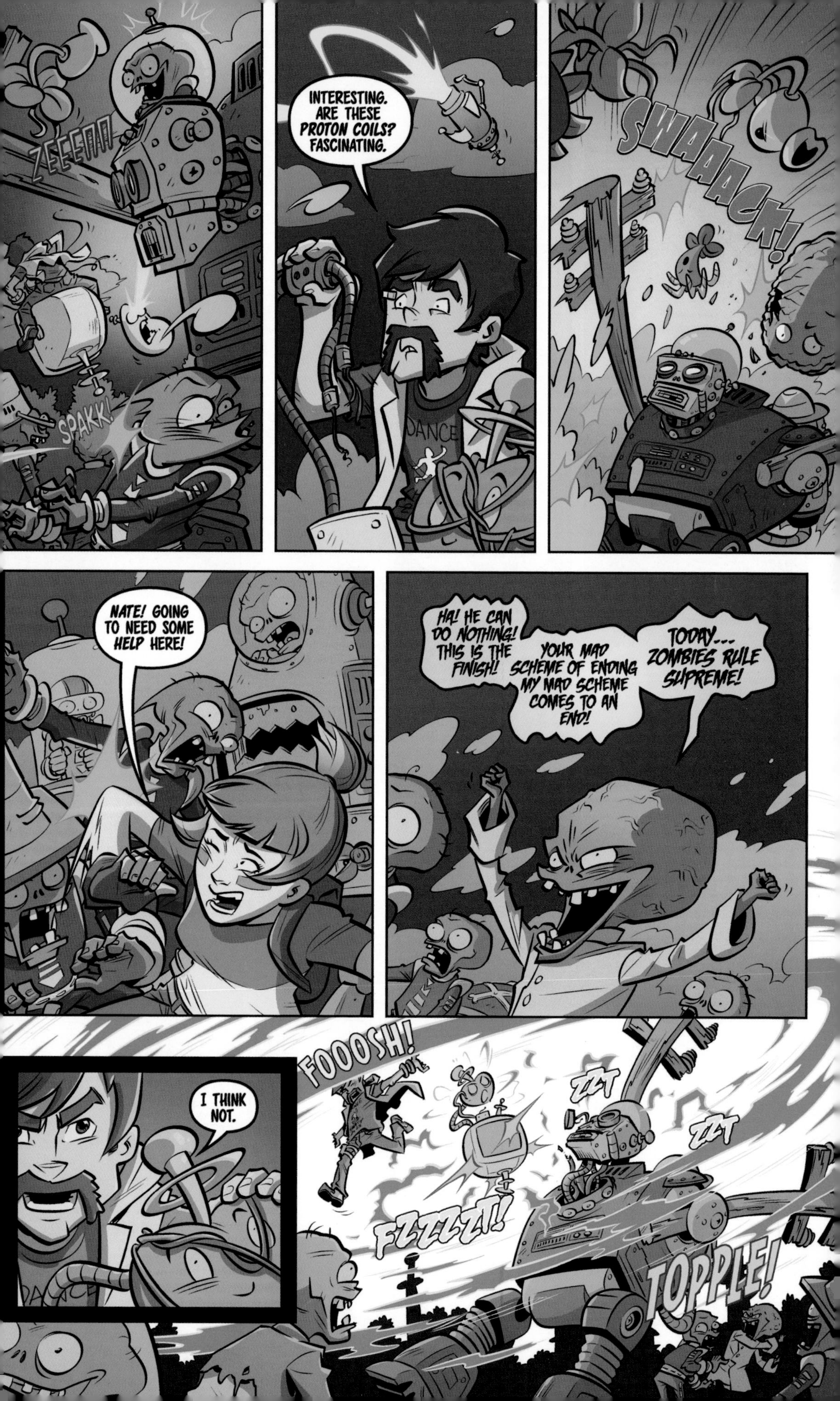
ZEEEEMM
SPAKK!
INTERESTING. ARE THESE PROTON COILS? FASCINATING.
DANCE
SWAAACK!
NATE! GOING TO NEED SOME HELP HERE!
HA! HE CAN DO NOTHING! THIS IS THE FINISH!
YOUR MAD SCHEME OF ENDING MY MAD SCHEME COMES TO AN END!
TODAY... ZOMBIES RULE SUPREME!
I THINK NOT.
FOOOSH!
ZZZT
ZZZT
FZZZZZT!
TOPPLE!

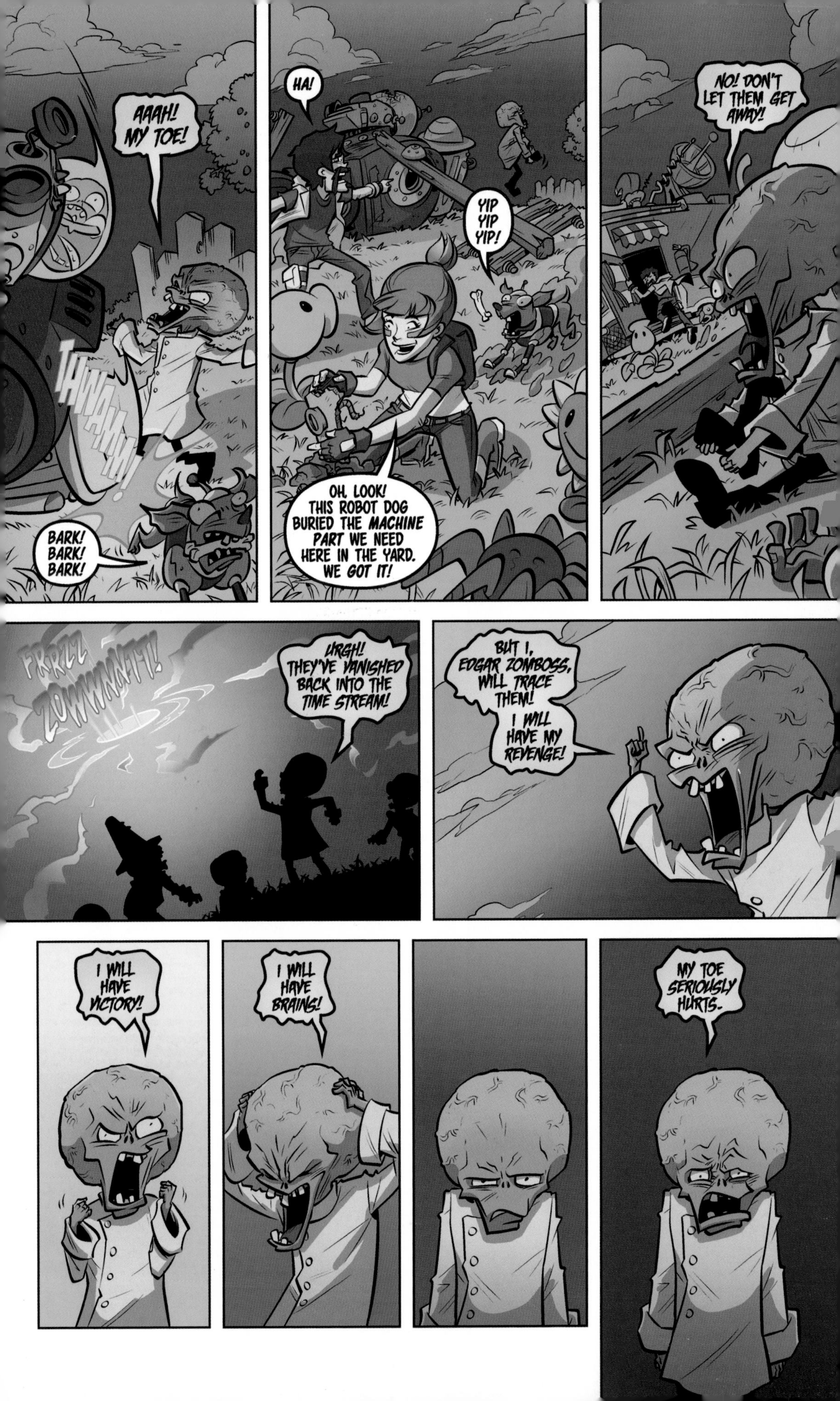

AAAH! MY TOE!
THWAMMM!
BARK! BARK! BARK!
HA!
YIP YIP YIP!
OH, LOOK! THIS ROBOT DOG BURIED THE MACHINE PART WE NEED HERE IN THE YARD. WE GOT IT!
NO! DON'T LET THEM GET AWAY!
FRRZZZ ZOWWNNFFT!
URGH! THEY'VE VANISHED BACK INTO THE TIME STREAM!
BUT I, EDGAR ZOMBOSS, WILL TRACE THEM!
I WILL HAVE MY REVENGE!
I WILL HAVE VICTORY!
I WILL HAVE BRAINS!
MY TOE SERIOUSLY HURTS.